Clint Faraday Mysteries
#17
A Long Way to Fall

A tourist falls off a small cliff and dies. As a companion is explaining what happened, Clint remembers the spot. He's explored there.

The man fell into that dry stream bed, then over the lower fall area, then onto the road and across to end up by the bay?

That meant he had to roll uphill and under the guard rail at a very specific spot – where the heavy brush would have stopped the fall.

Right! And I have this bridge in San Francisco I'll sell cheap!

Clint Faraday Mysteries
#17
A Long Way to Fall
(c)2011 & 2018 by C. D. Moulton

This is a work of fiction. Any resemblances to actual persons or events is purely coincidental.

Clint Faraday Mysteries
#17
A Long Way to Fall

Contents

About the author

CD was born in Lakeland, Florida. His education is in genetics and botany. He has traveled over much of the world, particularly when he was in music as a rock rhythm guitarist with some well-known bands in the late sixties and early seventies. He has worked as a high steel worker and as a longshoreman, clerk, orchidist, bar owner, salvage yard manager and landscaper – among other things.

CD began writing fiction in 1984 and has more than 115 books published as of this time in SciFi, murder, orchid culture and various other fields.

He now resides in Bocas del Toro and David, Panamá, where he continues research into epiphytic plants. He loves the culture of the indigenous people and counts a majority of his closer friends among that group. Several have "adopted" him as their father. He funds those he can afford through the universities where they have all excelled. "The Indios are very intelligent people, they are simply too poor (in material things and money. Culturally, they are very wealthy) to pursue higher education."

CD loves Panamá and the people. He plans to spend the rest of his life in the paradise that is Panamá

- Estrelita Suarez V.

CD is involved in research of natural cancer cure at this time. It has proven effective in all cases, so far. It is based on a plant that has been in use for thousands of years, is safe, available, and cheap. He has studied botany, and was cured of a serious lymphoma with use of the plant, *Ambrosia peruviana*.

Information about this cure is free on the FaceBook page, Ambrosia peruviana for cancer. CD asks only that all who try it please report on its effectiveness on that group.

For new readers of the Clint Faraday Mysteries, I will occasionally put a note explaining the series.

Clinton Faraday was a PI in Florida until he retired and moved to Panamá. He found far more interest in Panamá than he ever did in the states. He discovered the freedoms that were being more and more restricted in the states were here, and that the people were more "real" and honest, overall.

He was specially attracted to the lifestyle of the Ngobe Indios, the indigenous people in the area. His interest and caring were returned to the point he had become the secon person in history to be declared Ngobe.

His cases were almost always involved with murder.

He ws fascinated with the difference in the law on the comarca, and the practicality of the leaders.

He is becoming far more pragmatic. Not everything is cut-and-dried, and it is better that some be deported and barred from returning than housing and feeding them foe twenty years.

In many of the books, the ways of the natives are explained. To know the people was to love them. They were the best people in the world.

A few were the worst people in the world.

Clint Faraday Mysteries
#17
A Long Way to Fall

Prologue

"... were on a little rocky cliff up there to look out over the bay. You can see all the islands from up there. Jac told us about it – he's from France. We met him at the Barco Hundido, in Bocas – and we decided to climb. It's really high. It took half an hour to go just a few hundred meters!" the somewhat attractive blond backpacker, Suzanne Lizette, from Sweden, said to the regular group sitting on the balcony at Peter's Place in the Hotel Iris, David, Chiriqui, Panamá. She was telling about the accident in the mountains above the road from Almirante to Chiriqui Grande. One of them had fallen off a small cliff near the top, slid into a ravine and ended up in the mangroves on the edge of the bay 350 meters below.

The regular group was Jon, Jeff, Dick, Doug, Ralph, and sometimes, Clint Faraday, retired PI from Florida, who had more and more interesting and diverse cases here since his retirement, six years ago. He had proven himself to the police in Panamá, and they sometimes asked his assistance in difficult cases. After all, they are a pragmatic group, and Clint had thirty plus successful years experience as an investigator when he moved there.

"Paul and Erik were above, Lawrence and I were behind about five meters, Robert and Liam – he's from France, and knew Jon there – were just behind us, I think. Annette and Helene were behind them – we were going two together – Gus and Chastity were next, and Lars was behind. We would go a short distance and stop to rest, so we would change, sometimes. Someone new to talk with.

"When we started across that little rift mesa, Lars called that we must be extra careful because the rocks were loose, and to slip there might make you fall more than ten meters into the trees below. Lars is experienced in mountain climbing, so we all followed his advice at all times.

"Annette and I were first there. We did find it to be difficult going. The gravel would slide, but it seemed safe enough. The ledge is more than a meter wide.

"Lawrence and Helene were together, I think, next. We changed at the last stop, so weren't the same as when we started.

"Liam was with Chastity and Lars ... I don't remember. It was so bad. Everyone was in a group just there, except that Annette and I and were only two meters or less ahead. We all had to watch the path very carefully, because of the loose rocks. I don't think anyone could tell the police where anyone else was with any certainty. A lot of it fell when we moved. It's that stuff they call tosca here, and keeps sort of peeling off the side of the mountain all the time.

"There was some kind of loud noise, like a bird or something, from below. Right on or by the highway. We thought it may be a toucan, because it sounded just like a Quetzal bird in Mexico, and we all went as close to the edge as we dared to look. The road is almost straight down, there.

"I remember hearing Lawrence yell, 'NO!' and he was falling off the path. It was so bad, because the small stream was exactly under him, so he wasn't stopped by the trees only a meter or two away. He was rolling down the rocks and we were all screaming, then it was silent.

"We raced back down as fast as we could, but it took more than ten minutes to reach the road. He wasn't there, and we could see most of the stream bed. He wasn't there.

"Liam said there was blood on the road. Maybe someone found him and was rushing him to the hospital, but Lars said anyone who found him would certainly call!

"Liam followed the blood, and it went across the road. It was, I don't know, in patches. Liam said he was rolling, and had gone on across the road. Maybe he was semi-conscious, and had wandered.

"We went across, and saw some blood on the grass. He had rolled across and fallen down into the ravine, then down into the mangroves by the bay.

"Lars and Liam stayed on the road to wave down anyone who came. A truck stopped, and they called that they were going for the police. There's no signal for a celular there. Liam went, and Lars stayed. A bus stopped, and the people waited until the girls came back to the road. We were crying and scared. Lawrence was all twisted and bloody – it was horrible beyond conception!

"The police came, after about fifteen or twenty minutes that seemed like months."

"I know that area," Clint said. "A friend and I went along there several times. He does botanical research. I think I know where you're talking about. It's about three hundred fifty meters from that to the water, almost straight down. The angle meant he fell and rolled about three hundred meters."

"That was a long way to fall!" Jon exclaimed.

"No. It was a long way to be pushed," Clint countered. Everybody looked surprised. Suzanne was standing, mouth agape, showing shock.

"How..?!" she cried.

"I know that place. It simply could *not* have happened like that.

"You may have been in shock, and may not have noticed a few very telling points. That would be natural."

"But ... but the police said ... I mean, they came and checked absolutely everything and said it was unfortunate, but obviously an accident!"

"It obviously wasn't an accident if you know a couple of things about that place," Clint replied.

Chapter one

Clint thought for a moment about what the girl said in the restaurant. He knew the minute she described what had happened that no one fell exactly in that small place and didn't end up on the road. He wouldn't have rolled across the road and at an angle that would make him fall into the one small ravine that would allow the body to reach the bay. It was displaced from where the little rain-stream fell next to the road about eight meters, and slightly upward.

The strange bird call said a lot. It explained, to Clint at least, that someone was waiting there for the body. That someone rolled it up to the ravine and pushed it over. The call was to let someone else know the conspirator was there and ready. That one could be below and close on the road, under the lip the stream fell over and couldn't be seen from the ledge.

Clint was on the bus for Almirante, just past Chiriqui Grande. The spot of the "accident" was about forty kilometers ahead. He talked with Ernesto, an Indio friend, until he got off at the 46KM marker to go on out to Tierra Oscura. When Clint saw the yellow tape by the road, he called, "Sparate!" and got off. It was early, he had nothing else to do, so what the hell?

He walked back to the tape, and noted the small spots of dried blood on the road that led from just below the stream fall to the little ravine.

The body rolled under the low guard rail? It was only eighteen inches high, and there was small brush crushed where the body went under. The body fell on the road, rolled 10 meters, slightly upward, went through that brush under the rail and into the one two-meter wide spot where it would end up by the bay?

Uh-huh! And then Count Dracula stepped from the copse of heliconia, chuckled evilly, and flew off across the bay!

Clint went to the base of the trail, scanned it a bit, then went to the other side of the fall area and made his way to the dry streambed. He carefully checked among the rocks, finding a small pocket knife and a celular. There were a few odd coins. Those were all items that would fall from his pockets as he rolled.

The celular was a mess, but the SIM card could be read in any Mas Movil phone. It might tell him something.

He puttered around a bit more, finding nothing, then went to the road in time to flag down the next bus for Almirante. He was in Bocas Town at four thirty. He went to the police station and spoke with Sergio Sanchez, the head of the unit there. He hadn't been in on anything to do with the accident. Clint told him what he'd found, and gave him the celular. Sergio called for a Mas Movil phone and put the chip in. The phone had been used to make five calls out. The five were to only four numbers in the directory. The oldest was only two days ago.

"Bought a cheap celular here to use while in Panamá, then he would give it to the Indio kids or something when they left. Standard practice among backpackers who will be here a month, then move on," Sergio said. "The names in the directory are Lars, Bob, LF, ZH, and Chas.

"Where was the celular?"

"In the streambed where he rolled above the road. That little rain run-off cascada. No water, unless it's raining above."

"That little run-off fall not far from Pastore? A body fell off the top of the fall and rolled into the little drainage ditch to the bay? Bullshit!" Sergio exclaimed.

"My reaction, exactly. I was wondering why the police investigators didn't see that little detail from a hundred meters!"

Sergio called and spoke to somebody in the Changuinola station. He was told the police weren't there to investigate, because there were ten people who witnessed it, and it was ruled an accident. The police recovered and transported the body to Changuinola. It was to be cremated tomorrow, and the ashes sent to Sweden.

"I order a complete autopsy. CSI complete," Sergio demanded. "That was no accident! It's not even possible a body rolled ten meters uphill and through that heavy brush under the rail. It was murder. We have ten suspects instead of just ten witnesses."

"Eleven," Clint corrected. "At minimum."

"Eleven? Ah, yes! Someone was on the road to push the body into the ditch. The trouble is, we don't know the name of number eleven.

"We will!"

"I noticed the whole bunch were wearing those tight Spandex things every time I've seen them. Were they wearing that stuff up there?"

"Hmm. According to ... yes. They always wear that kind of thing when they go out for climbing or surfing or those kinds of things. Most are blue and white, some are green and yellow, some are other colors."

"Well, I think maybe another little thing fell into place with that bit of information. It could be important."

Clint talked a minute more, then went to his house on Saigon Bay, checked over his e-mail and phone messages, then went across to his neighbor, Judi Lum, to catch up on the gossip. He told her about the so-called accident. She said she'd heard a little, but didn't have any details. Just the normal gossip.

She would get the details. There was no one like her to find little things that turned into big things very quickly.

Clint went back to his place, where he took his boat out to Bastimentos to visit friends, returning at dusk to clean up and go to the Lemon Grass for some excellent Thai food. He talked with a number of people there, and at the Toro Loco, then went across to the Barco Hundido when it got started at about ten o'clock. Six of the backpackers were there. Four had gone to David, but would be back the following day. He didn't learn much more, but now had met six of the eight remaining people.

He also met Jac ("Oye ahm Zhok DUmon") Dumond. He wasn't impressed, though the slick gigolo-type was certainly trying his very best to impress everybody. He did mention that he knew that Lawrence Swenson ("LAW-rahnz SVEN-sohn") who had died over on the mainland. Their families knew each other. They were among the, like his own, elite in Europe.

"Elite pig farmers!" Yveth, a girl Clint knew in Bocas Town, remarked, just under her breath. Clint grinned. She grinned back.

Clint went back to the police station to see what Sergio dug up. The complete autopsy wouldn't be done until tomorrow around noon, if they didn't find anything new. He had a list of suspects that included Jac Dumond, the French man who had suggested the place who Clint met at Barco Hundido.

Jac Estrange Dumond, 26, France, traveling alone. Cancun, Mexico, Managua, Nicaragua, San Jose', Costa Rica, Bocas del Toro, Panamá. 2 wks. Cancun, three days, Managua, 2 days, San Jose'. Four days so far, Bocas del Toro. Police record, Paris and Versailles, France, for minor fraud 2009. No felonies.

Paul Sontag, 24. Erik Marks, 24, Lawrence Swenson (victim), 23, Belgium, Sweden, Mexico City, 4 days, Bocas del Toro, Panamá, four days.

Annette Johnson, 24, Helene Ingrid Wolz, 24, Switzerland, Sweden – same

Gustav Borsen, 23, Lars Larson, 27, Chastity Norstedt, 24, Norway, Sweden – same

Robert Robertson, 25, England, Sweden – same

Liam Fontaine, 27, Suzette Lizette, 27, France, Sweden – same

They met in a club in Echols, Sweden in person, though they had been corresponding for some time over the net and with Skype. The trip was planned for three months. All are from "good" European families and are independently secure financially, being in the computer site design business. All speak English, French, Italian, Spanish, as well as native language, though most of the families travel extensively and have holdings in various countries. Most wealthy; Larson, Lizette, Marks, and victim. Least secure (though substantially); Fontaine, Robertson, Sontag.

There are no police records on any of them, except for very minor things typical of teenagers the world over, though those families do not garner publicity, and records can be expunged by wealthy people, much as happens in

Panamá.

All are popular, to one degree or another. All follow the surfer crowd and backpacker crowd. All are athletic and adventurous.

Clint read it over. Not a whole lot.

"See anything?" Sergio asked.

"One small possibility. Not much, to overstate the case."

"I'll have to wait for the autopsy data to finish building a theory," he complained. "I wonder how differently the two of us will see this. What do you think it's about? Any ideas?"

Clint thought seriously for a moment. This was a very unlikely victim. Of all in that crowd, he would seem to be among the three who wouldn't end up murdered, in any likelihood he could imagine – overlooking the fact that was a purely statistical theory.

"I think I just got one," Clint replied slowly. "It's a cloud seen through a dense fog. Speculation one hundred fifty percent."

"Please, Clint! You are my dearest friend! Don't *do* that! You are *not* poetic!"

Clint gave him the bird.

Chapter two

Clint decided, seeing this didn't make sense the way it was reported that it happened, it didn't make sense. Something was drastically out of kilter here. He had to talk with these people individually to even come up with a theory. Suzanne Lizette sounded almost rehearsed in the Iris. She was nervous in a way that didn't quite fit with what she was saying. She said she was from Sweden, though she was from France. Liam Fontaine was from France, but they seemed to be together. That Jac Dumond character was from France and they – at least Fontaine – knew him.

Well, the group traveled together since Sweden, so she could have simply meant that. All of them had seemed nervous in the Barco Hundido, but that could well have been because of a bad experience. Backpackers wouldn't have a place they could stay until the shock wore off. They were the pack mentality, and would stay together for comfort.

Judi came to the door and said she had talked with a few people, but didn't learn much. It was mostly the typical backpacker chatter. There was a bit of a dispute at the Mondo Taitu, a popular surfer bar. "That French guy couldn't pay his tab, after buying a round for the bar. He claimed his pocket had been picked. He could get the money in the morning at the bank. Some friends said he was good for it so they paid, and he'll pay them back today."

"Liam Fontaine?"

"No. The greasy one. Jock or whatever. He woo-

DAUNT try to run out on a tab! Not some little fifty dollar no-THING! He ran tabs in PairEEE for hundreds of Eur-OHs and there was nev-AIR a probLEM, c'est certain-MOHnt, non?"

"Yeah. I talked with him last night at Barco Hundido. Whoopee-shit! I got the impression he was a lot of talk and not much action."

"Ronaldo, your Indio friend bartender, said that talk walks. Pay stays. He could find another place to hang out.

"Those girls are scared half to death of something. They stay close, and are jumpy. I think they know one of them pushed that guy off the cliff, and they're afraid they might be next. I don't think they have the least idea of who it could be. Suzanne was telling them the police said it wasn't possible for it to have happened the way they were told and the way they reported it. They think all but one of them are telling the exact truth, as they know it."

Clint nodded. It could very well be that only one of them had doubts at the first that it was an accident. One of them knew better. That was certain!

Clint decided he was going to Boca del Drago on the early bus. He was at the Golden Grill, and the girls in the group were waiting with their surfboards for it to come. He had about twenty minutes, so listened to the gossip from the group there. The talk was about the murder. Tom (who Clint simply couldn't bring himself to not dislike. He could usually be neutral about people, but not him) was expounding on a theory that they had been smuggling drugs around the world and it caught up with them. They probably crossed the wrong supplier, and this probably wouldn't be the last accident one of them had. He had it on good authority that they were under investigation. His good friend in the state department said they were to be watched every inch when they were in town.

"What state department would that be?" Clint asked innocently.

"Why, the only one I would know about. The US," he answered condescendingly.

"You're full of shit! None of them have ever been in the states," Clint replied sharply. "You'd better read up on the slander laws here. You can end up in the pen for three years for spreading that kind of crap about people! Maybe you'd better learn to put your mind, assuming you even have one, in gear before putting your alligator mouth in motion!"

This was the first time Clint had let the ass get to him to that extent. Everyone was staring at him in disbelief and amusement. Tom was hard to take. They were used to him, and tolerated him. Clint had enough of his attitude and "Better than thou" way of talking.

Tom fidgeted. He didn't know how to react to this bad turn of events. "I was just repeating what I was told," he whined. It was almost comical. He usually lectured with authority, now he was whining.

"Oh, so you can produce them if you're ever taken to court, and they'll admit it. That'll take the heat off you and put it where it belongs – on the ones who started the shit! I've talked with those kids, and they're mostly good people. They may smoke a joint – so do I – but they aren't into any kind of drug running or selling or anything else.

"There's my bus. Have a good day."

He nodded at the others and dropped a dollar for his coffee on the table and went out to help load the surfboards. There was an embarrassed silence from the table. He could imagine the backtracking from Tom as soon as he was gone. One at that table would wait anxiously for Clint to return to tell him what Tom said about him – which wasn't going to be complimentary.

The ride to Drago was pleasant. He talked with Helene and Chastity in the seat across the aisle. They were dressed in the regular Spandex suits for surfing. Clint said he thought he saw them with exactly the opposite suits on before.

"We exchange them. They're sort of property of the group," Chastity said. "I don't even think of it. When we're going somewhere for sport, I just grab the one on top of the laundered pile. We're not the type for matching accessories to the dress, if you know what I mean. We're not clothes horses. The nice thing about it is that one size fits all of us girls. Two sizes for the guys."

Clint said he had been to the place where their friend had fallen. It was a treacherous spot. The footing was very unstable there when it was that dry, and the tosca kept dropping pebbles on the path. It must have been a pretty horrible experience.

"The police say it wasn't an accident, but we were right there!" Chastity cried. "I mean, we weren't looking at him, but he wasn't ten feet from any of us. See, we heard what sounded like one of those toucans or something, and went to the edge to see if we could get a picture. I think he just got too close to the edge and the gravel gave way and he fell."

"He didn't cry out?"

"Yes. He yelled, '*no!*' as he went over," Helene answered. "Like, he started sliding and knew he was too close and yelled. I turned, and he was already falling. It was horrible!

"Look, I know everyone's curious, but can we talk about something else?"

"Oh! Sorry. Just, as you say, curious. I hear the waves are pretty good out from the pass. Should be a good day."

They talked about surfing in different places the rest of the way. Clint learned a little about their individual personalities. He had been right, in that they seemed normal people and not bad in any way. They were torn about the death, and were scared because the police claimed it was murder. They couldn't bring themselves to accept it, but it wasn't something that could be denied. All they could do was to carry on as always.

On the way back to Bocas Town, he asked what Lawrence had been like. He apologized, and said he was an investigator in Florida, and couldn't stop acting like one for very long.

"He was very nice. He was from a good family. We traveled for a couple of months together, and we all liked him. He was a very quiet type, and wasn't the easiest person to get to know, but he wasn't too very difficult, either," Annette replied. "He had some trouble a couple of times when his ATM card got damaged and he had to go to the bank for money, which meant waiting three days for the transfer from his folks. He was terribly embarrassed by it. He'd never had any trouble with money before, any-where in the world. His family is in a very high income level. I think they will be terribly hurt by this."

"Yes," Suzanne said. "All our families have had some losses with the markets being so unstable the past several years, but we were never hurting for anything. We all have reserves."

"I heard Liam's family was very hard-pressed," Helene said. "Of course, that might not mean the same thing to us as it would to other people who aren't so fortunate. When I'm hard-pressed, it only means I have to eat in four star restaurants instead of five.

"I sound terrible! I'm not really like that! I'm not a snob! I'm just so confused by this thing!"

"We're all still in shock," Chastity agreed. "I suppose I sound like some kind of freak. I'm just reacting and, I'll admit it! I'm scared! What if one of our group really did kill somebody? What if we figure out who? Would that mean we have an accident, too?

"I try not to think about it. I don't want to figure it out. I just want to go home as soon as I can arrange it."

"You can't go?" Clint asked. "I think that's what I'd do."

"We have to stay until the police finish what that police captain said is the preliminary report," Suzanne replied. "He says we are all suspects or material witnesses. He's really nice, and says he won't hold us in cells. We had to promise to let him know beforehand if we went anywhere. We told him we were going to the surfing beach. He said we could go anywhere on the island or Bastimentos or Solarte or Carenero. He meant if we went to the mainland or David or Panamá City or somewhere like that. He's a lot easier on us than on the guys, but that's because he would know that it would be one of them who..." She shuddered.

"Sergio? Yes. He tries to make things easier on every-one, but he's also a stickler about the job. You do *not* want to get on his bad side!"

"Liam's friend, Jac, has already gotten on his bad side, I think," Chastity said. "He was really giving him a hard time about something. Jaq, sorry Suz, can be a real ass."

"Don't be sorry! I say the same thing, but Liam grew up in the same places, and they've been friends for years," Suzanne said sourly. "He's a creep! He simply doesn't fit with us! I don't see how Liam can't see through that phony! I don't see why Robert paid that bar tab last night. I'd have let him stew. He's always broke, and always has an excuse. Larry would sometimes bail him out, according to Liam. Larry didn't like him, at all. I've heard him say Jac is the type who leaves a trail of grief anywhere he goes. He's good for a debt, but you'd think he'd budget things a little better. All of us have reserves, but we all also watch our money carefully. If things get worse, we don't want to have to go to work or anything. We *are* spoiled rotten, but we also try to be human. We're raised to respect certain things."

"I think Jac knows something about Liam. Maybe he knows something about Larry, too," Chastity said. "I think they bail him out because he knows things. He's around too much, and is a phony. I just feel it!"

They agreed. They didn't try to put on a front as being anything more than they were. Jac had one front or another anywhere he went. Clint was getting a bit of an idea from listening to them. They chatted about different things, then. Clint was mostly left out of it the rest of the way home. It seemed very telling that these people, only one of whom liked Jac, would bail him out. It also seemed he was around a lot more than the report from Sergio hinted. Clint wondered.... Did the wrong one get pushed over that cliff? How could that have happened? Was it Jac on the road? Did the wrong body come tumbling down that ditch, he panicked, shoved it on over, and ran?

This one just wouldn't come together. There was something behind it that never came out.

Clint was going to have to dig hard and deep.

Chapter three

"I learned that Frenchy didn't go near the bank today, but that no one seemed to notice or care," Judi reported. "I suppose that group doesn't think fifty four dollars is worth worrying about. I think that one's just following the group around for a free ride. I asked at the Barco, and Wanda said he left his wallet at the hotel and the one they called Larry, the dead one, paid it, and said to forget it. He pulls a 'damaged ATM card' routine at the Mondo two nights later? Uh-huh! A leech."

"I'm getting the same idea, but there seems to be more to it than that."

"Blackmail? I kind of got that idea from eavesdropping on three of the guys at the Muralla at lunch. He came in and asked Robert for fifty dollars until he could get to the bank. He hadn't bothered yet? Last night he promised, first thing, then he doesn't do it and even gets fifty more?

"Robert looked mad as hell, but didn't say anything. He gave him fifty. Liam and Gustav were there, and didn't even say hello to him. Liam's supposed to be the link, because he knew him in France, but doesn't even say 'hello' when he comes in to hit Robert up?"

Clint nodded. It was falling into place a little better – but why was Lawrence dead, then? It should be Jac! Could he have something strong enough that he could force someone else to kill a friend?

Clint was going to look up Dear Jac. Maybe accidentally happen to run into him somewhere and remember seeing him at the Barco.

That happened sooner than he'd hoped. He was on his

way to the police station to ask Sergio to make a more intense search of Dumond's past when he saw him go into the internet café across the street. He smirked and went in to find all the machines were occupied, Jac was sitting, but there were two ahead of him.

"Oh! You're that Jack. From the Barco the other night. I'm Clint. We spoke."

"Ah! Oui! I rememBAIR well!" Clint almost flinched at the overdone accent.

"It looks like about twenty or thirty minutes. Want a coffee? My treat!"

"Certainmont! Merci!" They went out and to the restaurant at the Bocas del Toro Hotel. Clint said he forgot to bring his laptop today. They could use the free wireless in the restaurant.

"You were with those attractive European girls, I remember," Clint said. "That whole group seem nice enough people. It's too bad their friend ... well. That can ruin any vacation suddenly and definitely. I was talking with the one, Chastity, I think, on the bus to Drago. She said it was a horrible experience, but her friend would want them to carry on. They didn't have anything else to do, really, so they would stay until they could go back home. The police won't allow them to leave the country until there's a determination or something. Very practical people. Swiss, I think."

"No. SveDEN. They are vair-EE nice people, I think. I know Liam, one of them. We were raised in the coun-TREE in Frahnce, you see. We are both of vair-EE good family.

"I fear that I am, how do you say? The blackest sheep of my family. I travel and have fun, they accumulate mon-

EE.”

Clint noticed that the accent was an on-off kind of thing. He would be speaking in a rather normal slightly accented English, then suddenly the overdone part. His phoniness was the repulsive thing about him. He would probably be average to moderately likeable if he’d drop the facade.

“Yes. They seem upscale, but remain good people to be around. So many of the wealthy, particularly European and American, can’t talk about anything but money and the stock market and so forth until you want to puke. Life’s got to be about more than that.”

“It is true. It is the way they are raised. If you were among those kinds of people, people with vair-REE much mon-EE, you would probably do the same, yes?”

“Oh, no! I’m quite wealthy. I just don’t let it control my life. I use the money. I don’t allow it to use me,” Clint replied, with a laugh. “Money’s not good for anything unless you use it for something good, I always say.

“You are a surfer?”

“But, non! I fear I have little ability at the sport. I like the people, and they are my age, with many interests the same.”

Judi came in and glanced at Clint, who excused himself and went to say hello and quickly tell her he wanted to impress that creep with his money, so play along with it. He led her to the table and introduced her. She smiled and put on her semi-airhead act. She seemed distracted, and Clint asked what was the matter.

“Oh, it’s the clinic. The one we’re building on Cristobal. They have to make a big fill where a sort of cave underneath fell in. The school on Popa and the clinic in Tierra Oscura. Problems all at once. (These were all projects Clint had instituted with funds from some of his cases. He seemed too often to end up with millions of dollars he didn't want, so built schools and clinics for his Indio friends.) It wouldn't be so bad if they were spread out, but things just don't go that way, here in Panamá. Feast or famine and devil take the hindmost.

"Clint, I know it's asking a lot, but could you advance us three million? You already dedicated the money for this, but we need it now, not in four months. I've put in one million, and Manny put in one, but it taps me out for the next month or so, and I do want those projects finished so we can do the thing out in Cusapín."

"Why the hell didn't you ask me earlier? You know there's no limit on those projects!

"Excuse me for doing business this way, Jack. I didn't expect ... here. I'll give you a note for Juan, at BNP. He'll give you the transfer and I'll go in later and legalize it."

"Do you need more? I'll make it for five. That should give you a buffer.

"Judi, when these things come up, come to me the first thing. Please!"

"Oh, Clint. We really do hate to always keep begging and imposing!"

"Judi, I started these ideas. It's part of the deal that you come to me." He scribbled a note and handed it to her. She said she would go straight to the bank, stood, and said she hated to come in and run, but this was important. Maybe she could stay next time.

Jac had sat there, dumbfounded, through this. He stammered a goodbye and stared at Clint. "Five million dollars? Just like that?"

"What? Oh. There's fifteen million set aside for those

things. She always hums and haws like she's asking for a handout. Hell! They're my projects, anyway! She's not begging to ask me to give out the funds that are marked for those things! I'll never understand people. I never will understand them."

"But ... five million, and you write a little note to the bank? They'll give her *five million dollars* because she has a note from you?" The accent was gone. Wow!

"Juan knows all about the projects and who's involved. She didn't really need the note. She could go in and tell him to give her the money for my projects." (True. Judi was administrator for the projects, as were several friends. The money was in their names as much as Clint's. It was money Clint got for solving cases he was helping the police with. Most of it was because crooks had put his name on things to try to hide them from the government or from other crooks. In two cases they were killed by those other crooks while the money was in Clint's name – that he didn't even know about, in one case – and it became his. He wanted enough to get by, and had always spent what he could to help the Indios. It was natural for him to use the money that way.)

Jac seemed stunned for a minute more, while Clint acted like he didn't notice. He was soon back to normal, and said a couple of things, then the accent started again, so Clint knew he had thought of a plan.

"Ah! I have off-TEN made donations to such wor-THEE causes, myself. I am more restricted in amounts, but would vair-EE much like to fund two vair-EE excel-LAUNT causes in Frahnce, but my parents do not aGREE, you see. They wish to have the mon-EE for the sake of hav-ING mon-EE. It is vair-EE sad!

"Ah! But you do not wish to speak of mon-EE! We will discuss oth-AIR things – such as that vair-EE pretty laid-EE by the wat-AIR there!"

They chatted about women for a few minutes, then headed back to the internet. There was only one machine available, and Clint insisted Jac take it. He said he was late already, and wanted to get to the bank, then he'd go home and use his comp, there. He went around the corner to find Lars and Gus talking with Suzanne and Annette outside the Toro Loco. He greeted them, and Annette said she saw him sitting at the hotel with Jac. "Be careful! He's a snake!"

Suzanne seemed mostly embarrassed at the remark. Lars nodded slightly, and Gus didn't react. Clint said he didn't seem the type anyone could trust far. Maybe it was the phony accent that kept changing and coming and going.

"That isn't the only phony thing about the ass!" Annette said. "He's a snake!"

Clint agreed, and said he had to get on to the bank and home. Maybe he'd see them around later.

"I hope you didn't let Jac know you were going to the bank," Annette remarked cynically. "He'll follow you and try to con you out of your last fifty!"

"I know the type, very well. I have quite a lot of experience with them here. He's welcome to try." He waved and went on. Judi was waiting near Las Brisas, and they walked on to Saigon Bay and home. Clint went into his house and worked on the computer awhile. He called Sergio and asked that Jac be investigated very carefully.

"He didn't kill Swenson. He wasn't up there with the group."

"I know. I think he was on the road. I think he pushed

the body into the cleft and ran."

There was a silence, then, "So he didn't do the killing, but he was part of it. I think I see where you're going with this."

"I think Swenson's body wasn't the one he expected to see falling off that cliff."

Chapter four

Clint cleaned up at six and went to town. He had dinner at El Ultimo Refugio and chatted with friends. His nutty musician/ botanist friend was there with Curtis and Rob to play music. Paul joined them, and it was a good night, until about ten, when Clint said he had a date of sorts and had to go. He went to the Barco, then to the Mondo Taitu. He found Paul Sontag, Erik Marks, and Robert Robertson at the Rip Tide, staring out over the water and talking with four of the local girls. The girls all knew Clint, and asked him to come over, seeing he was alone, to even up the table. He hadn't spoken with those three, so thanked Elena for the invitation and sat with them.

"Faraday? You're the big-time detective who's investigating us?" Robertson asked, with a smirk. Clint didn't care if they knew it, so nodded, and said he usually helped the police with people who spoke English. It saved having to use the local interpreter, who had a lot of other duties.

"And you're the one who came up with the theory that one of us shoved Larry off the cliff?" he asked. His tone wasn't the least bit friendly.

"No. Sergio, the police captain here, knows the area well, and immediately saw it couldn't have been an accident, though I imagine part of it was."

"Oh, really? And what made him come to that conclusion?"

"The body fell straight down onto the road, not in the ditch the fall runs into? It then rolled fifty feet uphill and under a guardrail with heavy brush growing there? It doesn't take a genius to figure something isn't right about that idiotic scenario."

"The police there didn't seem to see anything very odd about it," Marks pointed out.

"They weren't investigators. They were told to get statements from the witnesses to an accident and to transport the body to Changuinola. That's what they did."

There was a short silence. The girls tried to change the subject. All of them except Robertson seemed to think that was the best idea. Robertson said the police were stupid. So was anyone who would believe that kind of thing about any of them.

"I wonder why you're so adamant about this?" Clint asked. "Where were you – how close – when Swenson went over that little cliff in the one spot it would result in the long fall? When there was just some kind of birdcall just below that isn't like any call any bird or anything else makes around here? A call that was like certain birds found in Mexico and Guatemala?

"I was looking into it for the police, by their request. Now I have a personal reason.

"Why would anyone who was involved in anything like this be so insistent that it happened in a way it wasn't possible for it to happen? Hmm?

"I think the stupid one is at this table. It ain't me, Babe!"

"Maybe there are a few things you don't know!" he snarled. "Maybe several of us aren't what we try to make people believe! I guaran-damned-fucking-tee you none of us are lily-white! Larry was probably the worst of us, but no one would kill him! That's ridiculous! It would make better sense the other way around!"

"No one suggested you were innocents. I found a few things already. I think one of you, at least, is in cahoots with that French character in some kind of deal. It won't be a lily-white deal, by a long shot."

"Bob, what the hell are you trying to prove?" Marks demanded. "All you'll do is make them dig deeper into all our private lives. None of us are completely without things we'd rather not have known. Drop it or leave!"

Robertson got up and stamped out.

"I think I finally have one solid suspect I can concentrate on a bit more!" Clint said. "Enough of that! We have four beautiful girls, and just three guys. I kind of like those odds!"

The party was a bit nervous for a little while, then loosened up. They went to several places, then it broke up and everyone went where they had agreed, individually. Clint walked with Gloria and Marks part of the way. Marks said, much as he hated to say so, Robertson was right, in that he would be the one to kill someone, not the one to be killed.

Clint went home to get some rest. He felt he could put one more step of this thing together, now. It was a strange thing that could probably be cleared up if everyone would just tell the truth. Then again, he could see a reason none would dare.

He thought, then decided to accidentally drop in at the Barco Hundido. Jac would be out there, probably.

He wasn't. He was across the pass at the Splash. Clint went home, got his boat, and went to tie at the crowded dock. Jac was there, and drinking alone. He would leer at the single girls, who were studiously avoiding him. None of the others were there. He didn't have anyone to get anything from if he spent more than he had. Bummer!

Clint waved at him and went to talk with three girls

sitting at a table. He knew them, and bought a round of drinks. They chatted a bit, until Clint went to the restroom. Jac quickly came in and said, "Clint? I hate to have to ask, but I left my money at the hotel and don't even have the two dollars to get back to Bocas! Could you spot me twenty until tomorrow?"

"I don't have anything with me. I drink on a tab here, and pay at the first of the month. It's not smart to carry cash around these places at night. I'm going back across in about half an hour. I'll give you a ride. I have my own boat."

"Er, oh, well, thanks! I'll take you up on that! Wave when you're ready to leave."

Clint agreed and thought, *How strange! No accent at all! Vair-EE interesTING!*

He took Jac and two of the girls back to Bocas Town and went home. He was going to be busy tomorrow. He was coming up with a few little new ideas. He felt he was right on target to think Swenson was probably the wrong victim.

Who was the right one?

Jac was skating a bit close to the edge, himself. Robertson knew something. It could well be that they were afraid of each other for some reason. Jac, more than likely, because Robertson could prove he was the one waiting down by the road. It could be that Robertson was supposed to be the victim. It could be several things. Clint would have to eliminate all he could to get to it. He was beginning to believe the girls, most of them, didn't have a clue. The guys, most of them, knew, or thought they knew. There was a most definite scenario where they would stay shut up about it. He could end up drawn into another complicated case he didn't want.

No. This wasn't about that kind of thing. He would know by the way an outside character would begin to interfere before this point was ever reached. Tom's "information" was just something he thought up himself and yammered about because he didn't think anyone would challenge him. If there was any suspicion of any type about that bunch selling or transporting drugs, it would have come out with red flags all over the page on the net. The police nets would have been buzzing with warnings and advice. There was nothing there – nothing.

Which could be suspicious, in itself.

Chapter five

Clint finished his mug of coffee just as the comp dinged. He had an answer from someone!

It was from New Scotland Yard. Robertson was pretty much a normal sort. He had been in trouble over a girl, three years ago, who was supposed to be underage by about four months. They didn't pursue it, because the girl had instituted the affair and had lied about her age. She looked more like twenty five than seventeen. He had a difference of opinion about something or other with two men, but it seemed resolved. It was suspected that they were trying to extort money from him. The case was continued, with the strong caveat that he would pursue it if they ever again approached him with their veiled threats. It was quite possible it was attached to the underage girl, but that wasn't revealed by anyone. He was an independently wealthy man, having inherited more than half a million pounds and a small retail business from a grandfather. The shop dealt in highest-end imported sporting gear and returned him a very comfortable living, even without the inheritance.

More and less than he expected. It did give him something to investigate. He wanted to know who the two were who had tried to extort from Robertson.

There was nothing more, for the moment, so he went to town to listen to the gossip. Tom was there, saw him coming, and left. Suddenly. Jim and Paul said he said he was going to get even with Clint, but was such a blowhard wimp he decided to not be around to face another confrontation.

"He told us he was leaving only because if you provoked him again he would have to kick your ass on general principles," Charlie said, laughing. "I think you'd kick his ass in your sleep with your pajamas tangled up in your arms to where you couldn't move."

"I don't wear pajamas," Clint replied, with a grin. "Why can't that ass see he wouldn't always be in hot water if he'd learn to keep his mouth shut?

"Anymore gossip about the accident that wasn't any accident?"

"Not really," Paul replied. "Gisela tells me that French phony tried to get some more from the English one at the Taitu last night and got told off pretty good. I think maybe they've finally seen enough of him to catch on that he's a bum and won't ever be anything else. Maybe the dead guy was the one he needed to keep his act going, now he's gone."

"He makes me wonder," Clint agreed. "If he can't get anything more from them, he's in a hell of a spot. I think, from what I've seen of him, his parents won't send him money to get home. They'd rather he was around the world from them, somewhere."

"He whines," Paul said. "I never could stand a whiner."

They chatted about other things for awhile. Clint had one more piece of evidence for something. Jac had come back here from Carenero with Clint and gone to the Mondo Taitu for money instead of to the hotel where he didn't leave the money he didn't have in the first place. He was a pathetic sort.

Okay. He was waiting down on the road for someone's body to roll down that cliff. It wasn't Swenson. That meant it was one of the others. Clint originally thought it was Robertson, but he wouldn't have cut Jac's funds off if it was.

Would he? What had changed?

New scenario: Robertson had something that would prove Jac was on that road waiting. Now the blackmail evidence being used against him was useless, because Robertson had evidence of his own. That would mean Jac now had to try to start putting the screws to whoever the victim was supposed to be, otherwise he would end up in Panamá with no way home and his tourist visa running out, in a month or so. He had to live until then, even. This might suddenly get interesting in a completely different way!

Clint went to the police station. Sergio hadn't found anything new about any of them. He said those types of wealthy families could keep most negative publicity from ever being circulated in Europe as well as in Panamá. There were some things that seemed obvious as to who was what in this one, but there was always that little thing that denied it. The thing that seemed true from the first moment, that Roberson was supposed to be the victim, was negated before any more speculation showed he probably wasn't.

The scenario, as Clint now saw it, was that someone else was supposed to be dumped, but because of the clothes, or something else, the wrong one went over the cliff. The one who did the pushing saw the mistake immediately ... uh-huh. There was too much Clint didn't know. One thing he was fairly sure of: Swenson must have been wearing the wrong suit. That would mean that Larson, Borsen, Marks, or just possibly, Fontaine, were supposed to be the victim.

Were two of them wearing the same colors? Swenson and someone else? From the back, a mistake was very easy to make. From the back, there was just a solid color. The front had the different band or design or whatever. There were only two colors in the group from the back. Blue and green. That didn't change the scenario, it only modified it a little, and reduced the number of people he had to check closely. He would still check them all, but could use a bit of logic to direct his more intense concentration. He would see if anyone remembered who else had the same color back as Swenson.

He went back to his Saigon house to check his computer. Not much new. Chastity and Helene were definitely cleared. Annette probably was. Suzanne was proving difficult to trace, with any degree of certainty. There were conflicting things in her records.

Suzanne, Annette, Liam, Robert ... Sontag and Marks were off the list, for now, because of size. Jac wasn't a consideration for that part of it. He was the only one it could have been on the road.

Judi called to say that she'd learned a little. She'd run into the girls and had coffee and gossip with them. Clint said to come on over and he'd fix some gumbo. A friend had brought him some crawdads from the mountains. The Indios didn't eat them, and Clint had enough okra from his and Dave's yards to make a good pot of it. She said she had some spices that would go well with it. She would be right over.

The gumbo was delicious. Judi waited until they were sitting on his deck to give what information she had. It didn't seem like much to her, but she knew Clint saw things she didn't in this kind of thing.

"None of them like that Jac character. They say they think he has something on a couple of the guys or something, because he comes to them all the time for money, and never pays any of it back. The only one who defends him is that Suzanne. She's the only one I have any suspicions about. She's lying, sometimes. Her eyes give her away.

"Anyhow, they also think Lars and Gus are the only two in the group who have nothing to hide. They all admit that there are things they'd rather not have known, but none of it is anything some creep could hold over their heads. If Chastity's mom knew she'd been sexually active since she was barely thirteen she'd go through a bit of hell, but it wouldn't last long, because her mom had also admitted to her that she was no virgin when she met her father. She said her mother's big gripe would be that her name was Chastity. She had let the father pick the name, and had hated it all her life. That's why all she would ever call her was 'Honey' and 'Darlin,' unless she was being introduced to someone.

"Helene had a lesbian affair for a couple of months when she was eighteen. She decided that wasn't for her and hadn't done anything like it since, but her father would go ballistic if he knew it. They all had some experience with that in the surfer group, and said it was something they knew about each other, but they didn't much care, one way or another. Annette stole some jewelry from a guy who played her for awhile, then dumped her. She didn't need or want any money, she was just getting even. It was family heirlooms. He never caught on. He thought it was some whore he had there for two nights – which was when she learned he was just playing her. When she left, she told him he'd made the choice of what he wanted, and he could live with it. Get used to his type of girl being his type, because no decent girl would have anything to do with him the minute she learned what kind of asshole bastard son-of-a-bitch he was.

"Suzanne didn't admit to anything. Chastity told me later that she wasn't the type for girl talk. She always sat back, like she was doing there, and seemed embarrassed that they talked to each other like that. It was girl talk. We tell each other things we'd die of mortification if guys or family knew about. Everyone tells something about herself that's just for gossip and to trade little exciting stories. I told about slipping out for a few nights back in Taiwan and going to parties. They said that was nothing, but I told them they weren't Oriental, and didn't have an Oriental father. We all giggled about that."

"Did you?"

"What? Slip out? Of course! What girl didn't, at some time or other?"

"They say anything about the guys?"

"Only that Lars is such a big lovable teddy bear and the main one they could always count on in any bad situation. Erik is quiet, but has a temper. He beat the hell out of two men who were bigger than him in Hamburg when they put their hands on a girl he knew. She had been trying to avoid them, but they wouldn't leave her alone. He would have gone to jail with them if his parents hadn't brought a little pressure on the police to make them see it was only him defending a woman against two low-life brutes.

"Gus and Paul are good friends to have. They stick together with the girls when you really wouldn't expect them to, and when there wasn't any reason for it. They had both had opportunities with women they met that they turned down because the girls didn't have anyone to hang out with in some place, if they left. They couldn't make them see the last thing they would ask or expect is for that kind of loyalty. They were thoroughly capable of finding entertainment on their own, if they wanted. Robert isn't quite as popular, though they all like him. He seems reserved, and isn't as gregarious. He's a rock to cling to when things are really bad, though. He's a lot deeper than anyone knows. Paul is a lot like him.

"Liam is too French. The same as Suzanne. It seems a lot of the French are stand-offish with anyone not French. They're both embarrassed by Jac. Suzanne says he shows up where they are a lot too often, and she's sick to death of him. She can't understand why Liam doesn't make him leave them alone, even though they're lifetime friends. She thinks Liam doesn't really like him. He's just so loyal to people he doesn't know how to be honest enough to tell them they're a royal pain in the ass. She knows he resents the creep cadging money from the group.

"She feels sorry for him. She guesses she's as bad. She could tell him to piss off, but doesn't.

"It was girl talk, and I shouldn't tell you, but I know you need some kinds of stuff they talk about, and won't ever let them know I spilled my guts to you."

"It helps a lot more than you can know. There isn't any reason for them to ever know. It's for my own information."

They chatted a bit more, then Clint decided to go into town to check out a thing or two. His mental scenario had changed a little. Judi had come across again in ways she couldn't guess.

Chapter six

Robertson was sitting at a table in the Toro Loco, so Clint went in and asked if he wanted company.

"No, but that won't stop you. Have a seat."

"Not much of a vacation, huh?"

"Actually, it'll resolve some things. It's a nightmare, now, but it'll work out, I hope."

"With Jac?"

"Jac-off isn't a problem, like he used to be. He's never been the actual one behind ... him. We didn't know that until a few days ago."

"So. Swenson was the one behind it?"

Robertson studied him a minute, shook his head, and said, "So. You figured it out?"

"The blackmail bit? Yes. I was leaning toward thinking he was behind it, somehow. I just don't get why you chose that way to get rid of him."

"We didn't choose anything. He chose it."

"Now you lost me."

"So you haven't figured it as to who, you just ... but then you don't know why, either. I thought you had it figured, all the way, when you made a remark about him being the wrong one."

"I think, just maybe, I have it figured, now."

"Oh?"

"You found out it was him behind the extortion, and were about to expose that to the rest of the group. You were the one who was supposed to have the accident."

"Something like that. It was self-defense if I'd have done it. Pushed him over."

"He tried to dump you, and you turned it on him."

"He came up behind me when we heard the call and were going to the edge. He sort of lurched at me, I guess so he could say he slipped and ran into me if anyone saw. I managed to step to the side at the critical tenth of a second, he grabbed at me and went over. His alibi was going to be the loose gravel. That's what actually happened."

"Can you imagine the look on Jac's face when he came rolling down over that cascada?"

"I like to."

"Why didn't you just tell the police that he slipped on ... that's what you told them. That part was true, it's just what happened after he dropped onto the roadside that made you clam."

"I didn't know if the things he had on me would come out if I fingered Jac. I think a couple others figured that. We've been waiting for him to really come down hard. He didn't. I don't know why."

"Because Swenson had a deal with someone else. I'd say Liam Fontaine. Jac was just used because he's a sneaky little snake who can be manipulated by almost anyone. The cold one is ... I can't picture him being it."

"I can picture Suzanne being it. I can't be sure. If I could, I think maybe there *would* be a murder, then."

"No. Don't. You're in Panamá. Maybe we can find out and neutralize her ... or him. I'm still not sure. Can you tell me about it? I don't jabber, and I'll probably not give a happy shit. Maybe I can work back to the one it has to be."

"Nothing to lose, now. If anyone knows, I don't much care. It's a matter of whether they have any proof.

"Back in August oh four, I had a bit if a drug problem. Coke, mostly. Crack. I've gone off it, and get pretty hard against it, now. I know what it can do to you. You or I or anyone else aren't immune or strong enough to be sure it won't get us. I had a good stash in a backpack. The dogs would always find it, so I took a little powder and rubbed it into the outside fabric, just outside where the stuff was. They grabbed me three times because of the sniffer dogs, found the stuff on the outside, questioned me about it – I said I didn't have a clue. All our bags were in a pile in the trunk of the taxi or on the bus or whatever. There was always a little on a couple other bags, always on the outside. They let us go without opening the deodorant stick it was inside of.

"That would cause me a lot of problems, if anyone knew how it was done. It wasn't the kind of thing you could blackmail me over past a ten or twenty, now and then. If you didn't have proof of that, it wouldn't be good enough for a pound or dollar or whatever.

"The last time I used the method, in France, on my way to Belgium, they found the deodorant stick. Fortunately there was only a trace left in it. I was on my way to get a new supply set up. They questioned me for more than an hour about it, and I convinced them that it wasn't even the brand I use. I didn't have any idea of how it got in my luggage. The guard that let me go came into the hostel where I was staying that night and tried to put the screws to me. He'd checked, and knew that my family are all disgustingly rich, and wanted ten thousand pounds or he'd arrest me and expose what I was doing. We were on the balcony on the third floor, over a cobblestone street. I struck out before I thought and knocked him against the rail. He grabbed his pistol and was drawing it, still against the rail, I grabbed his foot and lifted. He fell over and landed head first on the cobbles.

"I didn't think anyone would know, but that was the moment I turned one eighty and have been against drugs from that moment.

"Then a picture of me on that balcony with the guard showed up. It's still out there."

"You've seen it? It's real?"

"I have a copy. If you don't have a connection, it's a picture of two people on a balcony."

"Can I see it?"

"We can go get it. It's in my backpack."

They went to the hotel. Robertson handed Clint a photo. It was fairly clear, and Robertson was easy enough to identify from it. The guard was in uniform. Clint studied the photo, and grinned. "We can neutralize this. If some slimy cop was into blackmail and got dumped when he tried to put the screws to somebody, big fucking deal! It's well-known by any cop anywhere that blackmailers are among the highest risk to end up dead by violent means.

"This thing is worthless. I can show it's a fake."

Robertson was staring in disbelief. "But...! HOW!" he cried.

"Look at the shadows. Look at the focus. On you and the guard, it's sharp and clear, and the small bit of shadow on the wall behind is to the left.

"Beyond the very close fringe, the balcony is slightly out of focus, and the shadows are nearly straight back. The picture of you and the guard was probably taken when you came in. The balcony picture was taken, then you and the cop were superimposed over it. This is a digital printout photo. If you check the pixelation on two parts of the photo, it will be different. That shows up easily with a magnifying lens.

"I wonder! Are the things the others are paying for as obvious and phony?"

"I always wondered why I had that sweater on on that balcony. I knew I wore it earlier, but could have sworn I didn't have it on that ... both are in bright daylight, too! It was dusk when it ... I was half-stoned, and thought it was just spotty memory. I didn't connect the time of day of the photos! *What* an *IDIOT*! I've paid those ... I've dumped about thirty thousand pounds to them, so far! What an *IDIOT*! I never thought to have authentication of the photo! I could have taken it to a shop in any town where I was. That kind of thing could be checked. I could have given a story that I wanted to know why my picture was taken at that spot where I'd never been, or something on the order."

"You wouldn't have to explain anything at all. Just say that you wanted the picture examined for authenticity. It's none of their business why."

"I could have seen it myself as easy as you did and I do now – except I almost panic when I look at it. What an *IDIOT*!"

"So. We have to know if Swenson knew it was phony. If so, I'll have Sergio close the case as 'Natural Causes' and you can forget it, except for helping me find who's really behind it. I want Jac tagged, and I want whoever he's been working with tagged."

"Natural causes?"

"Murder is a natural cause when the victim's a black-mailer. We look at things a bit different, here in Panamá."

"You know, I think I'm beginning to like the holy living hell out of Panamá!"

"It's a unique sort of place. Shall we see if we can find who's behind it? We have a couple of very solid and telling points to investigate."

"We do?"

"We do."

"I'm afraid I don't know much about detective work, except the bullshit on TV."

"What's one thing we can be damned sure of because of this phony photo?"

Clint received a questioning look. Robertson shrugged.

"Who was there to take the shots?"

"I'll be damned. Obvious."

"Most things are."

Chapter seven

Clint explained that he wanted everyone in that group's movements in August 2004 between the 6th and 7th known to the time they stepped in dogshit on the sidewalk in Podunkville, Alaska. Sergio shook his head and went to the computer.

"You have that here, or do you have to look it up somewhere else?" Robertson asked.

"We have your passports, every page. If they're from before then, it's there that we can trace further," Sergio replied.

"Oh, yeah!" Clint said. "You can mark Swenson's case as natural causes."

"I probably can, but why would I?"

"Because he was blackmailing several of us, and it really was an accident that happened when he tried to push ... someone else off that ledge," Robertson said. "The someone saw him coming and stepped aside. He really did slip on the gravel, because the person wasn't there to stop him."

"Why didn't you say so? I mean you ... oh. Blackmail. It will come out. That doesn't explain where the body ended up."

"Jac Dumond pushed it on over. He was there to get something from the desired victim's body. When the wrong body suddenly dropped at his feet, he panicked and pushed it on over."

"Ah! His boss fell out of the sky, not the, as you called him, desired victim."

"Something like that," Clint agreed.

"Hmm. Swenson was in France. Both Sontag and Marks and Wolsz were in Hamburg. Johnsen, Larson, Borsten were in Sweden. Robertson was in France, the sixth, and Belgium, the seventh. Fontaine, Lizette, and Norstedt were in France.

"So. You were the one being blackmailed, and the one who stepped aside at the critical second. If Clint says he believes you, I will believe you. It will be marked as closed."

"Wait just a little before closing it. I may need a bit of leverage and, very easily, I can make it look like we think the one who's really behind it ... who Fontaine knows! Let me try something! He's a whiny little wimp who can be scared into giving us what we need!"

"Ah! You have said he was waiting for the body on the camino. Someone will come forward who saw him there!"

"And even took a picture or three!" Robertson said. "I have fifty pictures with him in them. We can do to him what he did to me!"

"Shall we get some of those pictures and make a quick trip to the scene for some background?" Clint suggested.

They got his boat and went to close to the area to take a few shots with Clint's camera at the spot just below the little cascada. There had been rain in the mountains earlier, and water was coming over the ledge, so Clint took the photos from the side enough that the water didn't show. Then they took Robertson's memory stick, with hundreds of photos on it, to Clint's computer. They did an overlay that looked more real than the one with Robertson and the guard.

"I'll be thoroughly damned! Jac was waiting to get this flash stick! I always have it with me! There has to be something on it that Swenson was afraid of!"

"We'll find it. Later."

It took them more than three hours to get exactly the effect they wanted. When it looked just right on the screen, Clint had the printer make four copies of each of three shots. Jac was shown just to the side of the little cascada fall, then near the guard rail where Swenson's body was pushed over, then in two close spots just past the cascada.

Clint looked at the shots and the angles and rejected two of them.

"Why? They're perfect!" Robertson objected.

"The story that goes with them. Those two could have been snapped as a car passed. The one across the road, and the one twenty feet back, won't do."

"I see."

They worked half an hour more to put one shot of Fontaine in a particular spot in the background. Robertson asked why. The other two that they'd chosen were damned good.

"Because he had on this watch. The other shot showed him with a different one."

"You'd have to blow them up fifty times to see it!"

"I'm a detective. I saw it on these shots."

Robertson gave him a thumbs up.

"Oh, shit!" Clint exclaimed suddenly.

"What?"

"How do we show exactly when these were taken? It's not on the photos anywhere."

"That's easy! Any camera will put a date on your pictures, if you program it in. Look at those shots I took in Austria. I had the date on them."

Clint brought up the shots. There was a date in small block type on the bottom right in each photo.

"I think maybe ... did you date things very often?"

"No. A few times. I don't ... yes I do! That photo of me and the guard wasn't dated, so even that could have been explained as being another time!"

"But you have a dated picture of Swenson or someone that can crucify them. They definitely wouldn't be trying to knock you over if you had anything that could be explained away as being taken at a different time. It will make it a lot easier to find the one we want on that stick."

Clint brought his photos onscreen in the photo shop and used the text insert feature to place the block letter with the date in the lower right corner of the photos. He printed those out, studied the results carefully, and smirked. "Got the whiny bastard by the balls! Let's get this boat in the water!"

He checked again to be certain he had exactly what he wanted, then called Judi over. They got their story straight the way they wanted it, and she went with Clint into town. Robertson couldn't be there for this. It would look too much like a setup if he was there. They found Jac, Liam, and Suzanne in the Starship Surf Shop. Clint called Jac to the side, and he came over with Liam and Suzanne tagging along. "What eez eet you WAHNT? I'm biz-EEE!" He demanded.

"You're not going to have much to do the next twelve to fifteen years, so get unbusy!" Clint replied. Judi smirked at the ass, and patted her purse.

"Eeee? What are you talking about?" he asked in a whiny voice.

"You want your friends with you for this crap?" Clint

asked. "You're going to be charged with accessory to murder one. That's the same as the murder charge, here."

"I have no see-CRETS from my friends!"

"Drop the stupid accent!" Judi demanded. "It's never the same twice!"

"You remember the bus that went by while you were waiting for Robertson's body to drop over that ledge?" Clint asked.

"Bus...? I ... there were several cars and ... what are you talking about? What bus? Where? When? I was never waiting for.... Oh, God! Oh, God!"

"Shut up! Don't say another word to this one!" Suzanne cried. Liam yelled that Clint didn't have authority to say such atrocious lies here. He would demand that a charge of intimidation was brought against him.

"Before I even say what it's about?" Clint asked. "I think the accessories to murder've suddenly become three to one!"

Liam turned and ran out. Judi shook her head, and said, "Where the hell does he think he's going? This is an island!"

Jac looked as though he would start crying any second. Suzanne was standing with her hand to her throat and eyes wide. Sergio and another officer came to stand just outside. He raised an eyebrow and pointed to Liam as he ran down the street. Clint giggled. Judi looked disbelieving.

"It seems a woman, a tourist from Canada, was taking a picture or two of that little cascada Swenson's body dropped over as the bus passed. Two of those shots feature you." Judi said. "I really don't think you can explain that in the next twelve to twenty. Your friends can't explain their reactions before we even told you what it was about." She took the phony photos out of her purse and handed them to Jac, who just stared, and didn't take them. Suzanne took them, and said they were taken later when Jac went to see the place where Swenson had died.

"Uh-uh. They're dated. Lower right corner of the picture," Clint said. "The bus went by about ten minutes before Swenson's body dropped over that ledge. Jac here waited until there wasn't more traffic in view to make the call of a bird that's only found in Mexico and Guatemala. Mrs. Wright heard about it and when it happened when she came back from Costa Rica, and called me. She remembered that someone was on the road just there. She had pictures."

Jac whined a weird sound and took the pictures. He suddenly cried out, "There are false! I wasn't wearing that shirt *or* those trousers when I was there! I was wearing the blue Spandex ... Oh, God!"

"You are *so stupid*!" Suzanne snarled.

"And the two of you are under felony arrest on suspicion of aiding and abetting in a case of degree one murder," Sergio said. "Sanchez, go pick up that character who was running away when we arrived. Same charge.

"Let's go. It can be quietly, as I prefer, or with your hands tied behind your backs and my pistol in your ear. Your choice."

They went quietly.

Chapter eight

"We have to go through these dated pictures to find what you have that Swenson couldn't allow to be seen," Clint said. "It'll take time, I suppose. That's mostly the kind of thing detective work is about in the real world. Umpty hours of looking over papers or pictures or watching someone or something for days, then ten minutes of excitement – which almost never includes car chases or explosions that make Bikini look like a little firecracker, or crashing planes or boats. You arrest the suspects and they go with the cops to the police station, then you go home to wait for the several days when you sit in a courtroom after giving your five minutes of testimony.

"Whoopee shit!"

"I don't remember ever seeing Swenson before Sweden, just two days before we started this trip. That's what has me so confused."

"Sergio gave me a printout of his passport, and one of yours. I'm scanning them into the comp, where we'll take the places and dates from each and make a comparison list. Data correlation stuff. Saves ten hours of going through each thing, personally.

"It did occur to me that Swenson might not be the one we're looking for, here. It could have as well been Fontaine, Dumond, Lizette – any or a combination. First is what seems most likely. Swenson. I have the others' passport information if we need it."

"Sounds like a plan."

It took twenty minutes to scan and make the lists. Clint put a correlation order in, and found that Robertson had been in London for a two week period in 2009 when Swenson was in England, and for two days in 2008, they were both in France. He felt that France was most likely, because of the others from there being the ones running the blackmail scheme. June 11 and 12. Now was the time to minutely study any dated pictures from that time. None of them included Swenson. None were from France that were dated.

"Shit!" Clint exclaimed. "That means we have to go through all the pictures from that time to look for him!"

That was six hours. They found three that had who appeared to be Swenson in the backgrounds of two, and with an arm around Lizette in one with another couple with their arms around each other's waists.

"This proves he knew Lizette before this trip, but so what?" Clint mused. "We don't have a date, except that it was in a period of a couple of days. We probably can't prove a specific date from this, though you might remember it so we can work back to find what happened on that date in that place."

"I don't remember the exact date, but this one that shows him behind and to the side was three years ago in Paris in June. That will be either the eleventh or twelfth of June, two thousand eight. There was a person who was hit by that car, the red Renault, that I was taking a picture of. A woman. She had serious injuries that she later died of. She was mostly incoherent, but she did say she was pushed out in front of the car. I do remember that. It was in French, but I speak some French.

"That was the eleventh. I went back to London at eight o'clock next evening."

"You know something, Dude?" Judi, who was there for

part of the studying of photos, said. "I think just maybe there's a picture of him at that accident. I think just maybe that woman was pushed out in front of a car, and died, as a result. I think Swenson pushed her!"

"And the next day there's a picture of him with his arm around Lizette! Why did you take that picture?"

"It was a picture of Sam and Irene Arnold. They had just gotten married in that little chapel near Lourdes. The pictures were taken as they came out of the chapel there. They were just there at ... My God! What if Swenson and Lizette were married there, too? What if that's why they were in the picture at all? I can't think of any reason I'd take a picture of strangers. I didn't even get their names, though I imagine Sam and Irene would know them."

"On June eleven, two thousand eight, there was a murder. We can establish the time fairly closely, because of the accident. Swenson killed a woman by pushing her in front of a car in Paris, France. He married Lizette in Lourdes, the next day. We don't have a clue as to why he killed her.

"I think it's time to check with the police in Paris and the registry in Lourdes for things that happened on the eleventh and twelfth of June in two thousand eight. This just gets weirder and weirder!"

"You really sorta go for understatement, don't you?" Robertson asked, with a wry grin.

"Serg, we need information about some people in France on June eleventh and twelfth, the eleventh in Paris and the twelfth in Lourdes. There was an auto accident, where a woman was hit by a car, a red Renault, who died later, as a result of the injuries. We have to know everything we can find about that woman and the accident." Judi explained, at the police station. "We also have to know about who was married in Lourdes the twelfth."

"Learning little unexpected things about our little group of rich surfers?" Sergio answered. "I can't find much on the ones we have in the pen now. Those wealthy people have ways to keep things from getting into the records."

"I think we're about to learn one hell of a lot about a couple of them," Robertson said. "Like the fact that Swenson was married to one you're holding here, in Lourdes, France, on June twelve, two thousand eight. Like Swenson murdered a woman in Paris the day before he married her. Little interesting details about the private lives of normal people – don't apply here!"

"Clint's investigations seem to keep adding little things that surprise me no end," Sergio replied. "Paris, June eleven, two thousand eight, automobile accident, woman hit by red Renault, who later died. It'll take about ten minutes for the information to come in.

"Hmm. Marriage records for Lourdes June twelve two thousand eight. That'll come in fast. It's an automatic call-up.

"Marriages in Lourdes, France. Only three. Samuel Edward Arnold, twenty three, England – Glouchester, to Irene Marie Collins, twenty two, England – Hampshire. Giavani Marcus Bolinni, fifty eight, Italy – Norma, to Genivieve Georgette Sonnes, nineteen, Paris, France. Lawrence Bierce Swenson, twenty two, Stockholm – Sweden, to Suzanne Lizette Petite, twenty one, Floralia – France. So. Our victim was married to one of our suspects. We live and learn.

"Ah, yes! The automobile accident. Anne-Marie Sante-

Marta Swenson, thirty six, Paris, France, was hit ... suffered serious injuries from which she died two hours forty six minutes later. Her husband was in Bern, and came back, next day after being contacted through computer links. I'd suppose e-mail.

"So. She was the wife or mother – wife of Swenson. She dies, and he marries Lizette the following day. He was nowhere near Bern. The e-mail would reach him anywhere, and he could claim he was anywhere when he received it.

"Let's see. Made statement at scene, semi-coherent. 'She pushed me! It was her!' and 'I was pushed!' So. It wasn't him?"

"You have the memory stick with you?" Clint asked. Robertson handed it to him. He put into the USB port, and brought up the pictures of the accident. He magnified them until they began to pixelate, then closely studied them. There was one with the back of a woman showing that well could have been Lizette. She was wearing a showy gold bracelet with a distinctive set of alternated red, green, and black inset stones. Clint said he couldn't really be sure. Robert studied the picture, then exclaimed, "That bracelet! The wedding picture! She was wearing it there! I've seen her wearing it several times when we went out at night here!"

Clint brought up the picture of the two couples. Her right arm was around Swenson's waist and the left to the side. That bracelet was plain on her left wrist.

"I always thought she was one cold bitch," Judi said.

"She-esh! And all this time they were blackmailing me!" Robertson said. "If I'd seen these things then, those two would have been in the pen in France for the past three

years!”
    “C’est la vie!” Judi said. They all gave her the finger.

Clint picked up the papers by the printer and shoved them into an envelop and into his file cabinet.

Now for e-mail. One from Lars Larson. He wanted to thank Clint for exposing what had happened on their trip to Panamá the past month. It was chilling to learn you had been traveling around the world with a bunch of cold-blooded murderers and blackmailers.

His lazy gambling addicted brother was in deep trouble, and needed five thousand that he'd pay back as soon as he sold his Hummer he'd bought when he had the big win in Atlantic City. His expected funds hadn't arrived, and there was a chance the people who bought the place would default and blah, blah, blah.

Clint had turned him down for loans regularly for the past six years he'd been in Panamá. He wasn't about to enable a gambling addict. He had more money than he knew what to do with, but enabling someone with an addiction wasn't something he would spend a dime on. He sent back that the property in Florida still wasn't sellable (true), and he barely had the money to pay the taxes on it. He certainly wasn't able to send five hundred, much less five thousand dollars, at this time.

Dave, his nutcase musician/botanist/author friend, was staying in Cusapín with the Indios, where he was planning an extended botanical research trip along the coast eastward. Clint loved Cusapín and the people. There was an invitation to join them.

He might. He didn't have plans that never worked out here.

Sergio had e-mailed him a certified copy of the confessions and convictions of the surfers. Not much unexpected. Jac couldn't say enough about everyone else, and knew one hell of a lot of things. He, Swenson, Lizette, and Fontaine had been collecting evidence against them for the blackmail since they knew them. Most of what Sergio learned and found, such as photos and contracts and other papers, were somehow lost. Most of it was just things that would result in intra-family problems the victims would have to face. The evidence was no longer anywhere. They just *had* to get a more efficient system of keeping such evidence! If there was ever a need of any of it ... well, they'd make do. The stuff didn't exist anymore.

Clint grinned. He and Sergio agreed about most things. One thing was that evidence that could be used against a person in blackmail, unless it was for some major criminal thing, should disappear.

Robertson was planning on another surfing trip to Panamá, this time would be just him, Lars, Chastity, Gus, Annette, and Angela, a girl he'd met. They seemed to hit it off very well. It would be a great trip, and he promised he wouldn't bring any blackmailers or killers along for the next one. He had the geetus, and had learned his lesson. A very good private detective agency was going to investigate anyone he would travel with, very thoroughly, in future!

More power to you! Clint thought. He e-mailed replies to them, then went out on his deck. Judi was on her deck, and waved. She called that she wanted to go to Gary's new Mexican restaurant. Did he want to go?

He said yes. Twenty minutes. Be ready or he'd go without her!

She gave him the finger and laughed.

He cleaned up a bit, then he and Judi strolled into town. Ben and Earl, neighbors, joined them. They laughed and joked all the way to the cozy little restaurant, and found it was as good as people claimed. There were quite a few backpackers and surfers there. Once a place gets a good reputation in Bocas Town, they get a lot of business from the locals' recommendations.

They were relaxing and talking when a group came in. There were five people, two girls and three men. They seemed to be arguing about something. When they sat at the next table, Clint could hear them.

"Ah, but I am so VAIR-ee sor-EE ! I theenk a pick-po-KET took my mon-EEE at that Hundid-DO place! If you will lend to me the twenty five dol-LARS I weel repay YOU on the mor-ROW when the bank, she is o-PEN!' Oui?"

Clint paid the check, and his group went to the Toro Loco.

C. D. Moulton's works are available on most major outlets as printed or e-books. CD writes the CD Grimes, PI mysteries, the Det. Lt. Nick Storie mysteries, the Clint Faraday mysteries, the Flight of the Maita science fiction series, books on orchid culture and many others of many types. Mystery, adventure, intrigue, science fiction, fantasy, para-normal, mild erotica, and factual.